He had his mind made up.

He trusted his running a lot more than he did his passing.

All the same, he looped wide and held the ball up, looking like a passer.

He kept the fake until he could see that the defense was staying with the receivers.

Then he pulled the ball down and *darted* toward the goal line.

But a linebacker came up to meet him.

The two collided at about the 2-yard line.

Sterling lowered his shoulder and *smacked* the guy.

Best wishes!

Dean Hughes

Books about the kids from Angel Park:

ANGEL PARK FOOTBALL STARS

QUARTERBACK HERO

By Dean Hughes

Illustrated by Steven H. Stroud

Bullseye Books • Random House
New York

A BULLSEYE BOOK PUBLISHED BY RANDOM HOUSE, INC.
Copyright © 1994 by Dean Hughes
Illustrations copyright © 1994 by Steven H. Stroud

ANGEL PARK ALL-STARS characters copyright © 1989 by Alfred A. Knopf, Inc.
ANGEL PARK FOOTBALL STARS characters copyright © 1994 by Random House, Inc.

Library of Congress Cataloging-in-Publication Data
Hughes, Dean, 1943-
Quarterback Hero / by Dean Hughes
p. cm. — (Angel Park football stars)
Summary: Eleven-year-old Sterling Malone tries out for quarterback because
his father thinks African-Americans need to prove they can be leaders, but
Sterling isn't sure he wants to be a leader.
ISBN 0-679-84360-4 (pbk.)
[1. Football—Fiction. 2. Afro-Americans—Fiction.
3. Competition (Psychology)—Fiction. 4. Fathers and sons—
Fiction.] I. Title. II. Series: Hughes, Dean, 1943- Angel Park
football stars.
PZ7.H87312Qr 1994 [Fic]—dc20 93-8039
RL: 5.3
First Bullseye Books edition: September 1994
Manufactured in the United States of America   10 9 8 7 6 5 4 3 2 1

For Ted Goodman

QUARTERBACK
HERO

First Day

Coach Mahana was standing in front of the boys. He was wearing an old baseball cap with "Sidewinders" printed across the front. He had a clipboard under his arm. The boys were all sitting on the grass in front of him.

"Football is all about hitting the other guy harder than he hits you," the coach said in a deep voice. "If you're afraid of contact, you don't want to be a Sidewinder. Just go home now."

He waited.

But no one left.

Sterling Malone wasn't afraid of contact, but he was a little nervous about Coach Mahana. The man was huge, and he sounded *tough*.

Sterling was one of only two black kids on the

team. He had played a lot of sports. He was one of the stars of the Angel Park Little League baseball team. And he had become a starting forward on the town soccer team. But this was his first time to play football.

That was true for a lot of the boys. This was a league for 11- and 12-year-olds—the youngest tackle league in Angel Park. About half of the kids had only played flag football until now.

"All right. I need to know who wants to play what positions."

Sterling took a deep breath.

The coach got ready to write on his clipboard. "First off, who thinks he can handle the quarterback job?"

Sterling hesitated. He didn't really want to do this.

No one moved.

"Stand up. Whoever wants to be quarterback, stand up right now."

Sterling finally got up.

So did Kenny Sandoval.

Sterling had been afraid of that. He had the feeling Kenny would get the job. Kenny was one of the best athletes in town. Kids were used to thinking of him as a leader.

"What about you older guys?" the coach asked. "Don't any of you want to try? These two boys are both first-year players."

But no else stood up.

Kenny nodded at Sterling and gave him a quick little smile. The two boys were good friends.

"Well, all right," the coach said. "You boys walk over there." He pointed to the goal posts, off to his right. "Now, who wants to play running back or fullback?"

Derek Mahana, the coach's son, stood up. So did three other guys: Tucker Thatcher, Wes Hofmann, and Marco Zendejas.

Sterling wished he were with them. That's what he really wanted to play. But the competition would be tough for those spots too.

The coach kept calling out positions.

When he called for linemen, Sterling's friends Billy Bacon and Harlan Sloan stood up. Billy shouted, "*Yeah!* This is *my* sport."

Billy was rather short. But he was built strong, and he was a scrapper. Sterling knew he would be a tough blocker and tackler. Harlan was big for his age, so Sterling figured he would also be a good lineman.

The other guys who stood up were Jed Barlow, Bradley Udall, Lee Makosh, Brian Gonzalez, Matthew Kincade, and J. B. Bowen. They were all big guys—and strong.

Tommy Ramirez, a friend of Sterling's from school, wanted to be a wide receiver. So did Peter Winslow, Cosel Woodward, and Garrett Naylor.

Josh Briscoe and Brett Sanders, who were both good basketball players, wanted to play tight end. So did Michael Pitts.

Sterling was impressed. These guys were some of the best athletes in Angel Park.

Coach Mahana divided the team into groups. He had Sterling and Kenny throw some passes to the receivers.

It was late August, and *hot* in the desert country of southern California. Sterling was glad that he was only wearing shorts and a T-shirt. The pads would come out next week.

Kenny threw for a while. He was on target most of the time.

One of the assistant coaches was Josh Briscoe's dad. He showed the receivers how to run straight ahead, throw a head fake, and then cut left or right.

The receivers dropped a few passes, and

Kenny threw some that were a little off. But most of the time, the guys were making the catches.

When Sterling took his turn, he noticed Coach Mahana watching. Sterling knew he had to come through.

His first pass was long. He was too pumped up.

So he eased off. But this time he floated the ball. Brett caught it, but he had to come back for it.

"Zip 'em in there, Malone," Coach Mahana shouted.

And Sterling did zip the next one.

Cosel stretched hard and made a good catch. But the pass had still been a little long.

The coach walked away. Sterling wondered what he was thinking.

After the passing drills, the coach called the kids together again. He wanted to know what defensive positions the players were interested in.

Kenny and Sterling both wanted to be defensive backs. So they were competing again.

Sterling was sure the Sidewinders would have a good defense. The line looked powerful. The backs were fast. And the linebackers were some of the toughest kids Sterling knew.

Sterling wondered whether he shouldn't play mainly defense. Then he wouldn't have to worry about the pressure of trying to make it as the quarterback.

But he knew that wasn't one of the choices he was allowed. His dad wouldn't let him get away with that. Sterling had to *prove* to the world that black guys made good quarterbacks.

Sterling just didn't understand the way his dad thought sometimes.

At the end of practice the coach told everyone, "I have to say that right now you kids don't look like much. But you're just starting out. If you're willing to work—and I mean *work*—we might be able to make something out of you."

He took off his cap and wiped the sweat off his black hair. Coach Mahana had grown up in Hawaii. He had played college football. Some people said he would have made it to the pros if he hadn't torn up his knees.

"We don't have as many kids as usual. A lot of you will have to play both offense and defense. But that's not a problem. I can guarantee that you'll be in good shape after *my* workouts."

He hesitated.

"Our biggest problem is at quarterback. Sandoval and Malone have no experience at all. One of them is going to have to step forward and show he can lead this team."

Sterling felt his stomach do a little flip.

"But both of them have talent. In fact, this team is loaded with good athletes. Now it's my job to make *players* out of you."

As soon as the coach let the kids go, Sterling walked over to Kenny. "You looked good today," he said.

"I'd rather be a receiver," Kenny told him.

Kenny was a good guy—never a smart mouth. Sterling really liked him.

"Well, I'd rather be a running back," Sterling said.

"Why didn't you tell the coach that?" Kenny asked.

"Because of my dad—and my big brother."

"Your brother is a quarterback at the high school, isn't he?"

"Yeah. And my dad wants me to be one too. Is it the same with your dad?"

"Sort of. The coach told my dad that's what I should go out for. He saw me play basketball, and I guess he thought I could do okay."

"It sounds like you've got it made then."

"No. He just said I should try. He didn't say I'd get the job."

But Sterling wondered. Maybe the coach had already made up his mind.

"I hope you get it," Kenny said, smiling. "Then I'll see if the coach will let me play wide receiver."

"I don't know what I want," Sterling said. "I wish I could be a running back. But if I don't get to be quarterback, I'll be a big loser to my dad and brother."

Harlan Sloan had just walked over. "Boy, I don't envy you guys," he said. "The quarterback is going to take some heat on this team. Coach Mahana doesn't mess around."

Sterling and Kenny looked at each other. "Afraid so," Sterling said. Then he walked over to his bike.

Nate Matheson, his friend from the soccer team, was waiting for him.

"Well," Nate said, "I sure hope you've got time left for soccer. This coach is a crazy man. I'll bet he calls a lot of extra workouts."

Sterling was worried about that too.

He was getting to be a very good soccer player. He had even thought about staying with soccer and not playing football. He was built like a football player, tall and strong, but he had the speed and moves to be a great soccer player too.

But that wasn't an option. In the Malone family, all the guys *had* to be football players.

No—football *heroes*.

Dad had been a star running back in college.

Sterling's brother was heading for a college scholarship. He had been a great soccer player, but now, in high school, he was giving that up to concentrate on football.

And now Sterling had to live up to all that.

It wasn't going to be easy.

★2★

First Game

The Sidewinders worked *very* hard for two weeks.

The coach had handed out a schedule that showed only two practices a week. But Nate was right. Coach Mahana called extra practices. The kids ended up working out almost every day.

Coach Mahana had also scheduled three practice games before the regular season started.

On the night before the first practice game, he told the players, "Everyone will play. But here's the starting lineup."

He read off the offensive positions first:
Center: Brian Gonzalez
Guards: Matthew Kincade and Billy Bacon
Tackles: J. B. Bowen and Jed Barlow
Tight End: Josh Briscoe
Receivers: Cosel Woodward and Peter Winslow

Running Back: Tucker Thatcher
Fullback: Derek Mahana

Sterling held his breath. There was only one position left.

The coach hesitated and looked up.

"I still haven't made up my mind about quarterback. I'm going to play Sandoval in the first half tomorrow and Malone in the second half. I'll take a good look at both of them."

Then the coach read off the defense. Sterling heard his name. He and Kenny were both starting—at the cornerback spots. Harlan was starting at tackle.

Sterling didn't listen much to the rest. He was suddenly feeling twice as nervous as before. He had hoped the decision would be over. Now the pressure would only be worse.

And his dad and brother were planning to come to the game.

By the next afternoon, at kickoff time, Sterling was almost sick, he was so scared.

And his dad hadn't done one thing to take away the pressure. "You give it everything you've got," he told Sterling. "You can *take* that position if you really want it."

Sterling's brother, Reggie said, "I was in the

same situation when I was a freshman. But the other kid couldn't take the pressure, and I could. That's what it's all about."

That's what Sterling had to think about as the Santa Rita Bobcats kicked off.

Tucker Thatcher, the other black player on the team, received the kick and ran it back almost to the 40-yard line.

Good field position.

"All right, Kenny," Sterling yelled. "Go get 'em!"

Kenny ran onto the field. He looked sort of bulky in his uniform—which was an ugly shade of brown.

The coach said it was the color of the sidewinder snake. "I *like* an ugly color," he had told the team. "Let the other teams wear *pink*—or *baby blue*. I like the color of *mud*."

Sterling was standing next to the coach. He had heard him tell Kenny to start with a dive right—a quick handoff to the fullback. "Tell the boys to *pop* that first hit," he had said. "They need to show the defense who's boss."

Kenny ran to the huddle and called the play. Then the team charged up to the line.

Kenny bent over the center and shouted, "Down!

"Set!

"Hut! Hut!"

The snap came on the first "hut," and the offensive line drove ahead.

Kenny put the ball in Derek's arms. And Derek powered into the line.

And got *hammered!*

No gain.

Derek got up rather slowly. Then he trotted back to the huddle.

Sterling saw Kenny slap his hands together and say something to the offense. He was trying to be the leader out there.

The next play was a pitch to Tucker. Billy pulled from his guard spot. He and Derek led the blocking around the right.

But the end and the outside linebacker both got past their blockers and strung the play out.

Derek was finally forced out of bounds two yards behind the line of scrimmage.

Third and 12.

The defense would be looking for a pass. This was Kenny's first real test.

Cosel was wide to the right. Peter to the left.

When Brian hiked the ball, both of them broke straight down the field.

So did Josh, from the tight-end position.

The boys ran hard, as though they were going long. But all three broke off their charge about 15 yards down the field.

They curled back and looked for the quick pass.

Cosel was wide open. All Kenny had to do was hit him.

But Sterling heard a thud and looked back to see that Kenny had gotten *smashed.* A linebacker had broken through the line and hit Kenny just as he had set up to throw.

Harlan was standing next to Sterling. "Ooooh," he moaned, "Kenny got *stuck!*"

And Marco whispered, "These guys are ready to play."

Sterling thought Marco sounded scared. Sterling was feeling a bit the same way. He wondered what the rest of the Sidewinders were thinking.

It was fourth down now, so the coach sent Brett Sanders onto the field. Brett punted the ball away.

But he hit it badly—off the side of his foot. It angled out of bounds.

The Bobcats were going to get the ball almost at midfield.

"All right, defense," Coach Mahana yelled. "Get out there and show me what you've got."

Sterling ran onto the field.

"I'm sorry about that punt," Brett yelled. "Let's stop them right here."

Sterling knew the Bobcats' quarterback. Hugh Roberts. He was the star of every sport in Santa Rita.

And he was good, even if he was too cocky.

He shouted out the signals.

Sterling wanted to show that he could bang heads with anybody. But he was so nervous that his stomach kept churning.

And then the center hiked the ball.

Sterling saw Roberts hand off to Durkin, the running back. Durkin was coming wide on a sweep to the right. That was Sterling's side. He charged ahead and smashed into the fullback, who was leading the blocking.

Neither boy went down, but Sterling got knocked off balance. He caught himself and was about to charge forward again.

But then he heard someone scream, *"Reverse!"*

Sterling felt the play move away from him. He

spotted Tyler Brown, a Bobcat wide receiver, streaking back across the field.

The Sidewinder defenders had gone all out to stop the sweep. Now they were trying to recover and chase after Brown.

But he was turning the corner, and he had room to run.

Sterling took off, angling downfield. If no one else got to Brown first, Sterling thought he could cut him off.

Brown was racing down the far sideline. Sterling had a long run ahead of him.

But Sterling could fly.

He ran all out. He made up a lot of ground. And he almost got there.

He dove at the 5-yard line and managed to trip Brown. But Brown stumbled the last few yards and fell into the end zone.

Touchdown.

And it was the Bobcats' first play!

Sterling got up—slowly. He was still sort of dizzy from hitting the ground. And his shin had taken a shot when he hit the blocker, back upfield.

Wes Hofmann ran over to him. "We got *suckered*," he said.

Over on the sideline, Coach Mahana was yelling, "I told you outside people to stay home. What were you thinking about?"

Sterling was glad he hadn't made the mistake. Kenny and Bradley were the ones hanging their heads.

But the Bobcats were already lining up, getting ready to go for two.

"Short yardage defense," Brett shouted. "Let's stop them!"

And stop them, they did.

The Bobcats came with a quick handoff to the fullback. But Brett and Marco and Lee were all there to meet him.

And they *blasted* the guy.

The score was still 6 to zip.

But now the offense had to do something.

This time the kickoff rolled out of bounds. That gave the ball to the Sidewinders on the 35-yard line.

That was a good starting place. And they were ready to go.

The butterflies were gone now. Sterling had the feeling the Bobcats weren't going to outhit the Sidewinders on *this* drive.

On the first play, Kenny faked a handoff to the fullback, who charged the right side of the line.

Then he handed off to the running back, who angled back to the left on a "counter" play.

Tucker hit the hole—flying.

He popped through the line and burst 13 yards ahead.

First down.

The ball was almost to the 50-yard line.

The offense hurried back to the huddle. They got the play and then ran up to the line.

Kenny used a fake to the fullback again, but this time he dropped back to pass.

Cosel flew straight down the right sideline and took the cornerback with him. Josh, at tight end, ran straight ahead and then broke to the outside.

Kenny hit him with a pass just as he made his cut.

Josh caught the ball and turned upfield. And he broke it big. Almost 20 yards.

Now the offense was rolling.

Derek smashed straight ahead for four yards on first down. And then Kenny hit Tucker, coming out of the backfield, with a short pass.

Tucker made a great move, broke a tackle, and picked up another first down.

The Sidewinders were on the 20-yard line, and charging.

Sterling heard the coach send in a play with

David Bryner. Eighty-one pass. It was the same play that Josh had broken for the big gain.

But this time Cosel beat the cornerback and went flying toward the end zone.

Kenny went for it all.

But the ball seemed to slip off his fingers. It looped too high, too short.

And the safety got over in time to pick it off.

The big drive had suddenly crashed to a halt.

★3★

Sterling's Turn

The first half kept going the same way. Kenny did a pretty good job. The offense moved the ball. But something always seemed to go wrong.

The Sidewinders never did get a score.

Meanwhile, the defense got hard-nosed and worked over the Bobcats' offense.

So the score at halftime was still 6 to 0.

Coach Mahana was not pleased.

"This game is all about knocking people down," he growled. "And you guys are the ones getting banged around out there. I want to know—are you going to play football or not?"

"We're going to put 'em on their *butts!*" Billy yelled. A big cheer went up.

But Sterling thought the coach was wrong.

The Sidewinders hadn't been knocked around. They had made some mistakes—mental mistakes—but they had played hard.

All the same, Sterling's dad came down from the bleachers. "You guys have got to take charge," he told Sterling. "It's time to show what you're made of."

Sterling nodded. "We will," he said.

But the truth was, he was scared. He wished he could just stay on defense and let Kenny take the heat for not scoring.

Harlan kicked off. And he really got his foot into it. The team charged hard and made a good stop at the 18-yard line.

The coach told Marco to go in for Sterling at cornerback. "You concentrate on offense for now," he told Sterling.

But standing—waiting—only made Sterling more nervous.

The defense shut down the Bobcats on the first two plays. But then Marco let the wide receiver get open over the middle. The guy caught a pass for a first down.

On the next play the fullback hit the middle and took a hard crack from Garrett. The ball popped out of the fullback's arms.

Four or five guys dove for the ball at the same time.

And they ended up in a pile.

Sterling waited, and hoped, as the refs untangled the players.

And then Jed jumped up with the ball and waved it over his head.

Sterling started to charge onto the field, but the coach grabbed him. "I'll call the plays. We won't do anything fancy. Let's just push it in. Start out with the twenty-five lead right. That's been working."

On a "lead play," the fullback would smash through the hole first and lead the way for the running back.

Sterling ran to the huddle. He stood in front of the players and tried to sound calm and confident.

"Okay," he said, "We're going to *drive* it in. Strong right. Twenty-five lead right. On one. *Yo!*"

All the players returned the shout. *"Yo!"* They spun and charged up to the line.

Derek led the blocking. Tucker crashed in behind him.

But he only picked up about a yard.

Sterling turned and looked to the bench.

Tommy ran in with the play. "Twenty-nine trap," he said.

This was an off-tackle play. The blocker would let the defensive end through. But the idea was to "trap" him.

Matthew Kincade, the left guard, would pull from the line. He would cut to his right and hit the end as the tackle let him come through on purpose.

But everything went wrong.

Matthew hit the end, but he got knocked back. And a linebacker plugged the hole.

Thatcher tried to go wide, but he got tackled around the ankles by the cornerback.

The play lost a couple of yards.

Now the offense *had* to come through on third down.

The play the coach sent in was about what Sterling expected. "Split right. Eighty-two pass."

The wide receivers would both go long. Josh, the tight end, would run about five yards and then cut to his right.

"Okay," Sterling told the team. "You wide receivers have to beat the cornerbacks. I'll throw to the guy who gets open."

Sterling's heart was pounding. He had never thrown a pass in a real game. He knew from practice, however, how wild everything could get.

Spotting a receiver in coverage—with a rush on—was about the hardest thing he had ever tried to do.

The defense would be looking for a pass. They would be rushing *hard.*

As Sterling walked to the line, he took a deep breath. And then he barked out the signals.

He took the snap and dropped back five quick steps.

He spotted Cosel. But the cornerback was running right with him.

He tried to look left, but a Bobcat lineman had broken through a block and was charging straight at him.

Sterling turned and ducked. The big lineman went flying past him.

And then the middle of the line opened up. Sterling was too panicked to take another look for a receiver. He took off through the hole and shot upfield.

He was clear for a good 10 yards. He knew he had the first down. But then he faked the strong safety left and broke right.

A defender had an angle on him, but Sterling's speed was kicking in.

He blew by the defender and was *gone!*

As he cruised into the end zone, he felt something go wild inside.

He had *scored*.

He had done it.

He spiked the ball hard into the ground. Then he turned and raised his fists into the air.

At the same moment he saw a yellow flag go flying. "No spiking in this league," the ref shouted.

For a moment Sterling wondered about the rule. Would he lose the score? But the touchdown was still good. The penalty would only hurt his team on the kickoff.

Sterling could hear Coach Mahana, from the sideline, really chewing on him.

But right now, the crucial thing was to get the extra point.

Or in this case, to go for two. No one on the team was place-kicking well enough yet to try for one.

The play the coach sent in was a surprise. Sterling would fake a handoff up the middle. Josh, at tight end, would hold his block for a moment and then slip into the end zone.

Then Sterling would lob a little pass to him.

It was a great play for the situation.

And it worked perfectly.

Everything but the pass!

The defense took the fake and crashed into the line to stop Derek. And Josh was wide open.

But Sterling lofted his pass too long. Josh dove for it but couldn't quite reach it.

The score was still tied, 6 to 6.

Sterling ran to the sideline. He got an earful from the coach. "You've got to *concentrate*, Malone. The guy was *wide open*."

He didn't say one word about the run Sterling had made.

The Sidewinders were kicking off from the 20 because of the penalty.

And that turned out to be a big problem for them.

The kick was short and the Bobcats made a good return. They ended up starting their offensive series from the Sidewinders' 42-yard line.

"Malone, you better go back in at corner," Coach Mahana yelled. "Let's see you cover that wide receiver."

Sterling was glad to go back into the game— and get away from the coach.

The defense talked it up. They had to get tough and get the ball back.

On the first play they fired out hard.

The Bobcats tried to catch them out of position again. They tried another reverse.

This time Kenny stayed home. He met Brown in the backfield and knocked him for a four-yard loss.

That was more like it.

On the next play Brown ran straight at Sterling, and Sterling gave some ground. But Brown cut off his route and broke to the sideline.

Roberts hit him with a pass for a 10-yard gain.

The Bobcats still needed four yards on third down.

This time Brown ran the same route, and he was open again. But the throw went to the other side.

Another sideline pass. And Roberts connected again.

First down.

Sterling told himself he had to crowd Brown a little more. He couldn't let him have that much cushion.

So he crept forward a yard or two. And sure enough, Brown came at him again. This time Sterling was ready.

But Brown hitched, and then broke past Sterling.

Sterling spun, but he knew he was too late.

Brown was running down the sideline. He caught the pass in stride.

Sterling raced after him, but Brown was gone—for six points.

The Bobcats tried for two points again. And failed. But now the score was 12 to 6.

The pressure was back on the offense.

And Sterling was the one who had messed up. The coach didn't have to say anything. Sterling knew what he had done.

But the coach said plenty!

★4★

The Battle Back

Sterling felt more pressure than ever. He had to make something happen.

But the next drive didn't go well.

The Sidewinders picked up a first down on a pitch to Tucker. But then Sterling tried to pass. And he got sacked for a big loss.

Then a "motion" penalty sent them back another five yards.

The Sidewinders ended up punting from deep in their own territory.

At least the defense played tough. They shut down the Bobcats and forced them to punt after three plays.

And that's the way things kept going.

As the game moved into the fourth quarter,

and on toward the end, the score was still 12 to 6.

Then something finally went right.

Hugh Roberts tried a pass over the middle. The ball hit the tight end on the shoulder pad and bounced straight into the air.

Tucker was in the right spot at the right time.

The ball dropped into his arms, and he made a good run. When the dust cleared, the Sidewinders had the ball on the Bobcats' 39-yard line.

With about four minutes left in the game, Sterling knew he had to lead his team into the end zone.

This was his chance.

Sterling stood in front of the boys in the huddle. He tried to stay calm. "All right. Let's do it," he said.

The coach had called an option play. Sterling was a little nervous about that. He would carry the ball. And he had to decide whether to hand off to the fullback, keep the ball himself, or pitch back to the running back.

He walked to the line, got ready, and took the snap. He faked a handoff to Derek. Then he ran hard to his right.

He looked for a chance to cut upfield, but the

outside linebacker beat his blocker. Suddenly he was in Sterling's face.

Sterling hurried his pitch to the trail man—Tucker.

As Sterling went down he saw that his pitch was high.

Tucker leaped up and caught the ball, but all his momentum was stopped.

But he made a great move to shake loose from a tackler, and he broke into the open.

He got eight yards on a play that had been heading for a loss.

The next play was a handoff to Derek. He smashed ahead for four more yards.

First down, and the Sidewinders were now on the Bobcats' 27.

The end zone was getting close.

The coach called the option again—to the left side.

But Sterling didn't read it very well.

He thought he saw an opening, so he kept the ball. A linebacker closed quickly, however, and Sterling only got a couple of yards.

The next play was a pitch to Tucker—a sweep right. He picked up a couple more yards, but it was third and 6.

The play came in. Eighty pass.

All the receivers would bust straight down the field and then curl back.

Sterling had a feeling that Cosel was the one who would force his man deep and get open.

And so he looked to Cosel all the way.

And Cosel did get open.

But Sterling was *too* psyched. He muscled the pass, and it sailed high. Cosel leaped and got his hands on the ball.

But he couldn't bring it down.

So now it was fourth and 6 and time was running out.

Somehow Sterling had to keep the drive going.

Peter ran onto the field with the play. "Strong right. Tight-end dump."

It was the play Sterling had messed up before when he had missed the two-point conversion.

"Okay," Sterling said. "Josh, hold your block for a second, and then slip out. But make sure you get six yards downfield."

The team ran to the line. "Down!" Sterling called.

He *had* to do it this time.

"Set." He took a breath. "Hut. Hut. Hut."

He took the snap and dropped back. He had to wait—had to look long—and then dump the ball off late.

But the Bobcats were coming with a linebacker blitz. Sterling dodged to the left. He came up ready to throw, but the strong safety was all over Josh.

Sterling brought the ball down.

And now everything was turning into a blur, with white shirts all around him.

He ran to the right and took another glance downfield.

Josh had spun and broken away from his defender. He was wide open in the middle of the field.

There was nothing but grass between him and the end zone.

Sterling set his foot and fired. The ball spiraled like a bullet.

But the throw was too hard.

Josh jumped. His fingers touched the ball. But he couldn't make the catch.

The chance was lost.

The Bobcats took over on downs. And now all they had to do was run the time out.

The Sidewinders used their time-outs. They

tried to get another shot at the ball.

But it didn't happen.

The Bobcats hammered at the line until they got a first down. And that was it.

On the last two plays, Roberts just put his knee down. He only wanted to run out the time and take no chances of turning over the ball.

As the scoreboard hit zero, he yelled, "That's it, Sidewinders. You just got your butts kicked."

It wasn't really true.

But it felt true.

Some of the Sidewinders told Roberts to shut his mouth, but most just walked off the field.

Sterling felt bad enough, but then he heard someone behind him say, "Josh was *wide open*. All Sterling had to do was lob it to him and we had six."

Then Sterling got to hear Coach Mahana work the whole team over.

He was ashamed of them, he said. "You guys only gave about half the effort I want to see. And you looked like you forgot everything we learned at practice."

He paced back and forth in front of the players.

"We've got to do a *lot* more work on your basic

blocking and tackling skills. *Maybe* we've got a chance to be a decent team, but I didn't see much evidence of it today."

Sterling's head was hanging already.

But then the coach put on the final touch.

"We've got to find a quarterback who can get the ball to a wide-open receiver. If we can't do that, we don't have a chance to win—no matter how hard we try."

The coach announced an extra practice the next day. Then he walked away.

Sterling avoided everyone's eyes—even the guys who told him he had done all right. Once the crowd had cleared, he got up from the grass and walked over to Kenny.

Kenny looked as discouraged as Sterling felt.

"The quarterback has to take all the heat for everything," Sterling said. "It's not fair."

Kenny was holding his helmet under his arm. He wiped his shirt across his sweaty face. "It's hard to stand back there and throw when guys are coming at you from all sides," he said.

"That's right."

The two just looked at each other. "I don't want to be quarterback," Sterling said. "I hope he chooses you."

"I say, let him find someone else."

And that's what Sterling told his dad that night. "I want to be a running back. I don't like having to take all the heat when we lose."

But Sterling could see immediately that his dad wasn't going to give him any pity.

He slipped his hands into his pockets as he leaned against the door frame. He was looking into Sterling's bedroom.

"Sterling, that *heat*—as you call it—is just exactly what I *do* want you to take. It's experiences like that that make a man out of you."

Sterling was lying on his bed. He rolled his eyes and looked up at the model airplanes hanging from the ceiling.

Sterling's dad was an airline pilot. It was time for his "I have a lot of lives in my hands" speech.

"You know, every time I take off in an airplane, I have a lot of lives in my hands."

This was the one, all right.

"I could say, 'I don't want that kind of *heat*.' But I'd rather say, 'I can handle it. I'm a man.'"

"You don't have Coach Mahana chewing on you."

"Is that what's bothering you?"

"That's part of it."

"Well, I'll tell you what to do about that. You take it."

And that was the end of the conversation.

Sterling had been mad at the coach, but now he was twice as mad at his father.

And there wasn't one thing he could do about it.

★5★

Watch and Wait

At practice the next day, and all the next week, Coach Mahana used both Sterling and Kenny at quarterback. He didn't ask anyone else to practice at the position.

And neither boy stepped forward to say, "I don't want to play."

Both had talked to their dads.

Finally, on Thursday, before the second game was about to start, the coach called the two boys over.

"I've been riding you guys pretty hard," he said. "But you both have a chance to be very good, and you need to handle the pressure— even if it's coming from me."

He smiled just a little.

Sterling was shocked. The coach had never said anything like that before. The only thing he had ever done was chew, chew, chew.

"Sandoval, I think you have the edge right now. I'm going to go with you today. But Malone, if Sandoval messes up, you'll go in. That should add a little *more* pressure on you, Kenny."

The coach actually laughed.

"Coach?" Sterling said.

"Yeah?"

"If Kenny's going to be the quarterback, could I try out for running back?"

"Well, Thatcher is doing a good job in that spot. And I need a backup quarterback. What if Sandoval gets hurt?"

"I just always wanted to be a running back."

"I've got some backups at running back. I need you two where you are. And you'll both play plenty of defense."

Sterling nodded. But he wasn't happy.

"Malone, you might end up at quarterback. I don't know yet. Keep fighting for the job if you want it."

"Okay," Sterling said. He felt as though he were listening to his dad all over again.

Except—his dad came on even stronger when

Sterling told him that Kenny was starting. "I can't believe it. Have you really been busting your hump at practice?"

"Yeah, I have."

"Well, I doubt it. You don't even *want* the position. You're probably dogging it, just so the coach won't start you."

"No, I'm not, Dad."

Reggie was standing next to his father. "If the coach gives you a chance to play, you've *got* to come through. You have to look better than Sandoval this time."

So Sterling was right back where he had started.

He couldn't win unless he got the position he didn't want.

The game was against the Blue Springs Scorpions. Sterling knew the quarterback. He was a kid named Dave Weight, who had played third base on the Blue Springs baseball team.

The guy was big, and he was a good athlete.

In fact, from what Sterling had heard, the Scorpions had a great team this year.

As the game got going, however, Kenny looked a lot better than he had the week before. He seemed more relaxed.

On the first drive he handed off to his backs most of the time. But he made a nice run on an option play. And he threw a perfect pass to Peter, right over the middle.

The Sidewinders picked up some first downs and drove the ball deep into Scorpion territory.

But then Tucker got hit just as he took a pitch from Kenny, and he fumbled the ball.

The Scorpions recovered.

Sterling ran onto the field. He made up his mind to play tough defense and to forget everything else. He at least wanted to show his dad that he wasn't "dogging it."

And he got his chance on the very first play.

The Scorpions tried to run wide to his side of the field.

Sterling made sure that the play was a run— and not a running back pass—and then he *charged*.

He knocked the lead blocker down and went after the running back—a guy named Cooper.

Cooper tried to get around him, but Sterling was just too fast. Sterling ran him down and tackled him behind the line of scrimmage.

As he got up after the tackle, he heard his

brother yelling from the bleachers. "Way to go, Sterling. Way to *stick him!*"

Even the coach shouted, "Nice tackle, Malone."

Weight threw two incomplete passes after that, and it was fourth down. The Scorpions had to punt.

As Sterling trotted off the field, he yelled, "Okay, Kenny, get it in the end zone this time."

But the Scorpions had other ideas.

They had started rather flat. Maybe they hadn't expected too much from Angel Park after hearing about the game the week before.

But now the Sidewinders had the Scorpions' attention.

And the Scorpions began to sting!

On the first play, Kenny handed off up the middle. Derek got hit right at the line of scrimmage. As he struggled to break loose, two linebackers came up and *cracked* him.

On the next play Kenny faded back to pass. But the blitz was on, and he got chased out of the pocket. He pulled the ball down and tried to run around the end.

But he took a hard shot that knocked him out

of bounds three yards behind the line of scrimmage.

Third and 13.

Sterling figured the defense would be blitzing again.

The coach must have been thinking the same thing. He sent Garrett into the game for Cosel. "Tell Sandoval to run the middle screen."

The call was right. The Sidewinder lineman would let the defenders through. Then Kenny would pass the ball over them to the middle of the field, which should be left wide open.

The Scorpions came hard on the blitz.

Kenny faded back five steps—and then he dropped back some more. Four rushers were in his face.

The screen was setting up just right. He lobbed the ball to Josh, who had drifted into the middle.

But a linebacker must have sensed that the up-front blocking was too soft.

He held his position. Then he broke in front of Josh and stole the pass.

And he was off and running.

Kenny was the only one who had a chance to get him. And he gave it all he had.

But the linebacker had too much of a jump on him. He went all the way.

The Scorpions even had a good place kicker. He knocked the ball through the uprights, and the score was 7 to 0.

Sterling was mad. The defense had held them, and now the offense had given up a score.

But he wondered about something else.

If he had been playing quarterback, maybe the same thing would have happened. At least Kenny was the guy who had to listen to the coach this time.

And yet...maybe Sterling would have zipped the ball a little harder. Maybe he could have made the play work.

And right now Sterling would be the hero.

Quarterback was that kind of position. And now that he wasn't on the field, Sterling sort of missed the excitement.

After the kickoff, the offense tried to get a drive going. But the Scorpions were still giving them trouble. The drive bogged down after one first down.

At least the Sidewinders' defense was staying tough.

When the Scorpions got the ball, twice in a

row they had to punt after three plays.

Sterling was playing tough too.

Weight tried to throw to the wide receiver on Sterling's side. But Sterling covered the guy well. Weight had to look for someone else.

When the receiver tried to break past him, Sterling lost a step for a second. But with his quickness, he made up the ground.

Weight threw anyway, but Sterling reached out and knocked the ball down.

On the very next play the same receiver ran straight at Sterling and then curled back.

This time Sterling had given the guy a little too much room. But he reacted quickly and got back. He *popped* the receiver just as the ball got to him.

And he jarred the ball loose.

So Sterling was feeling good about his own game. He just wasn't happy about the score.

All the same, it stayed the same until the half and through most of the third quarter. And poor Kenny was getting chewed out by the coach the whole time.

Even worse, Sterling heard the guys on the sidelines.

No one seemed to say anything about the offensive line, or even the backs. It was always, "Kenny's gotta get going."

Or even, "Why doesn't the coach put Sterling in?"

Sterling wondered the same thing at times. But he wasn't really sure that's what he wanted.

And then it happened. The Scorpions had to punt again, and after the play, Sterling ran toward the sideline.

But the coach called out, "Malone, come here."

He told Sterling, "Okay, I want you to take over for Kenny. Start with a split right formation. Eighty-three pass. Let's open things up a little. And Malone, this is your chance to show me what you can do!"

Sterling heard a couple of guys on the sidelines say, "Good! Sterling's going in."

He also felt his heart begin to *pound*.

★6★

Sterling's Chance

Sterling talked to the guys in the huddle. "Okay. It's about time we put a drive together. Let's knock some people down!"

The players grunted their agreement. But Sterling didn't see a lot of confidence in their eyes.

"Split right formation. Eighty-three pass. On one."

"*Yo!*"

The players charged to the line. The tight end took his position on the right end of the line, and the receivers split wide.

Sterling was already nervous. But starting with a pass *really* scared him.

The right-side wide receiver and the tight end

would both go deep. They would take some coverage with them.

Then the other wide receiver and the running back would cut underneath the coverage, five yards downfield.

One of the them should be open, he told himself.

But Sterling also knew that Cosel just might blow past his man, and the team could get a quick touchdown.

And that's what he was thinking when he took the snap. He dropped back and looked deep.

But as soon as he released the ball, he knew he had done the wrong thing. The cornerback was all over Cosel, and the safety had come over to help.

He watched as the safety made a move to the ball. It looked like an interception.

Cosel saw the same thing. He jumped high and reached over the safety's shoulder.

He slammed the ball away, as though he were the defender.

Sterling was relieved. At least he hadn't turned the ball over. But he also knew he had made a dumb mistake.

He had made up his mind where he was going to throw the ball. Then he hadn't switched off when the pass was covered.

It was just so hard to think in the middle of all the action.

Coach Mahana was yelling, of course.

And Tucker came back to the huddle saying, "Sterling, I was wide open. I could have gained twenty yards—easy."

The next play was an option to the right.

"Come on. We've got to make this work," Sterling shouted. "Everybody *block*!"

Sterling barked out the signal and then took the hike.

He faked the handoff and ran to the right. He made a good cut, but he saw the defense closing in. He looked back and pitched to Tucker.

Tucker took the pitch and slashed ahead. He side-stepped one defender, twisted, and spun. And then he lowered his shoulder and took on a tackler.

It was a good run. He was close to a first down.

Third and 1—maybe less than 1.

The coach called the option again.

This time Sterling didn't fake. He stuck the ball in Derek's gut and left it there. Derek bulled ahead, took on two tacklers and kept driving his legs.

He made the first down with room to spare.

The Sidewinders were still on their own 36-yard line. But they had moved the chains. It was a start.

Wes came into the game for Tucker. He brought the play with him: "Split right. Eighty-three pass."

The same pass.

"The coach said to go to the running back this time."

Sterling knew that already.

This time Cosel got double coverage again, and Sterling looked deep. Then he turned and tossed to Wes, who was swinging out of the backfield.

Wes caught the pass in the open, and he sprinted over the 50-yard line before anyone caught him.

Another first down.

"Okay, we're rolling," Sterling told the offense.

Billy grunted, "These guys aren't *that* good. Let's put 'em on their cans."

The linemen liked that. *"Yeah!"* they growled.

The coach called the option again.

This time Sterling faked the pitch to Wes, and

then cut upfield himself.

He made a good move on a linebacker. Then he cut back toward the middle of the field.

He broke free. Now he only had to beat the safety. But the guy made a good open-field tackle.

All the same, the play had gone for 14 yards. The Sidewinders were on the Scorpions' 34-yard line.

At that point the third quarter ended, and the teams had to change ends of the field.

As the Sidewinders got ready to go again, Sterling could see that the players were starting to believe in themselves.

Billy was telling everyone that the guy he was blocking was a wimp.

The coach sent Tucker back in. He called for the option again.

"Let's break it this time!" Sterling told his team.

But the defense guessed right. The end beat his blocker and crashed over the line of scrimmage.

As Sterling came down the line, he had nowhere to go. He should have taken the loss, but he tried the pitch—too early.

The end dropped off Sterling and chased down Tucker.

Six-yard loss.

Second and 16.

Sterling was suddenly afraid. He had to make something happen right here—right now.

Peter brought the play in. "Fifty-two pass."

Both wide receivers would run at the cornerbacks. Then they would break to the middle on post patterns.

Sterling knew he had to stay calm and make a good pass.

He took the snap, dropped back, and set himself. Then he saw Peter bust past his defender into the open.

Sterling cocked his arm and was about to release his pass when he got hit *hard* in the back.

As he went down, he felt the ball slip from his hand.

His face mask slammed into the grass and pain shot through his back.

But he hardly knew it.

He was trying to scramble out from under the tackler. He had to recover the ball.

But the whistle was already blowing. And the

referee was signaling that the Scorpions had re-covered the fumble.

Coach Mahana was going nuts. "What are you talking about, ref? His arm was moving forward. That was a forward pass."

But Sterling knew better. He had fumbled, and the drive was dead.

He got up. Then he bent forward and tried to catch his breath. Pain was spreading up his back and into his shoulders.

Still, he was about to head to his position at cornerback when Marco ran onto the field for him.

Sterling walked to the sideline. He bent over again, with his hands on his knees.

The coach said, "Take a rest for a minute. We're going to get the ball back. And you're going to stick it in the end zone next time. You were on your way."

Sterling believed that, but he was feeling light-headed. And he was still having trouble getting his breath.

"You're not hurt, are you?" the coach asked, with no sign of any pity.

"No. I'm okay."

"Sterling, good job," he heard his brother yell. "You guys can still win this game."

But the Scorpions began a drive of their own.

After they picked up a second first down, the coach sent Sterling back in on defense.

He was still hurting some, but he put that out of his mind.

"Get tight on that receiver," the coach told him. "Marco was giving him too much room."

So Sterling watched the guy close. But the play went the other way.

The Scorpions ran a sweep—a running play with three lead blockers around the right end. The play picked up a few yards. Kenny made a good tackle to keep it from breaking big.

And then Weight tried a sideline pass again.

Sterling was ready.

He made a quick move to the receiver. Then he looked for the ball.

That's when he saw his chance.

Weight had floated the ball. Sterling cut in front of the receiver and made the pick.

Then he took off up the field.

The running back reacted quickly and got over in time to cut Sterling off.

All the same, Sterling had run the ball back to

the Scorpion 31-yard line. The Sidewinders were back in business, better off than before.

Sterling was excited. He would get it done this time!

But he tried the option again, and the defense was stacked for it. He got stopped for no gain.

With the defense expecting a pass, the coach called for a draw play.

But Derek got tripped up at the line of scrimmage and stumbled ahead for only about three yards.

On third down, Sterling tried to hit Peter with a pass over the middle. He got off a decent pass, just a little high. And Peter got hit as he tried to make the catch.

He couldn't hang on.

So now it was fourth down. The Sidewinders' great chance was slipping away.

But there was no use punting from inside the 30-yard line. If the punt went into the end zone, the Scorpions would get the ball on the 20 anyway.

Sterling knew the whole game could be riding on this one play.

Tommy came running onto the field. He told Sterling to run the eighty pass.

It was the curl pattern again. Sterling had to find the open guy and pick up the first down.

But as he took the hike, he saw the safety flying in from behind the line.

Safety blitz.

It was a gamble play, sending the safety after the quarterback from his position deep in the defensive backfield. But it was a surprise play, too, and it sometimes worked.

Derek was supposed to step up and block him, but he was late. The safety broke through.

Sterling spun away.

The guy got a hand on Sterling, but he slipped off. And Sterling kept his balance.

He looked up to pass, but pads were popping all around him. Then he saw a sliver of room in front of him, and he slipped through it.

A linebacker had a good shot at him. But Sterling made a quick cut left, and the guy slipped off his legs.

Sterling stumbled, then got his balance and shot ahead again. Then he cut back to the right, away from the cornerback.

He was flying now, angling toward the right corner of the end zone. He left the cornerback behind, but one defender was still in front of him.

The guy came at him, under control, ready to make the sure tackle.

Sterling set his foot and cut left, straight downfield. The tackler got an arm on Sterling but couldn't wrap up.

Sterling broke free and was *gone*.

He loped into the end zone.

The Sidewinders had finally scored!

★ 7 ★

Best Shot

Sterling had only a moment to celebrate before the truth hit him. The last play hadn't really been the big one.

The next one would be.

The team was still down by one point, 7 to 6.

The Sidewinders would go for two. And that could be the game.

Sterling liked the call. It was a roll-out pass.

He would sweep to the right and look for any one of three receivers. They would be trailing across the end zone.

But Sterling knew something more. If the defense stayed back and tried to cover, he would run the ball into the end zone.

So when he took the snap, he really wasn't thinking pass.

He had his mind made up.

He trusted his running a lot more than he did his passing.

All the same, he looped wide and held the ball up, looking like a passer.

He kept the fake until he could see that the defense was staying with the receivers.

Then he pulled the ball down and *darted* toward the goal line.

But a linebacker came up to meet him.

The two collided at about the 2-yard line.

Sterling lowered his shoulder and *smacked* the guy.

And then he spun and dove. He stretched out, holding the ball out over the line.

Then he rolled over to see a referee with both arms in the air.

Two points!

The Sidewinders had taken the lead, 8 to 7.

The Scorpions' coach was yelling, "That's all right. We still have time."

And Coach Mahana was shouting, "This game isn't over, boys. We've got to play some tough defense."

But somehow Sterling knew the game *was* over. He could feel it as the defense took the field after the kickoff. And he could hear it as the pads smacked on the first play.

The Sidewinders had worked hard to get this

lead. They weren't going to give it up now.

They *hammered* the Scorpions for three straight downs. Time was getting short, but the Scorpions were deep in their own territory.

Their coach didn't gamble. He called for the punt.

And Tucker let the ball bounce and roll, not taking any chance of a fumble.

The Sidewinders' offense charged back onto the field.

They kept the ball on the ground, pounded out the yardage, and kept the clock running.

They fought their way to two first downs, and that was it.

Sterling put his knee down and let the time run out.

And then he leaped straight into the air. "All right. We *did it!*" he shouted.

And the next thing he knew, he was being mobbed. He hadn't really thought of himself as the hero.

But clearly the players did.

Finally he began to realize that he had made the big interception to get the ball back. And he had run for the touchdown *and* for the two-point conversion.

Then why didn't he *feel* like a hero?

The coach gave him a pat on the back and

told him he had done all right. "But we still have a lot to work on," he added.

Kenny came over and said, "You got it done, Sterling. I couldn't do it."

And his brother told him, "You're the man, little brother. You're the quarterback now."

But Sterling wasn't sure about that.

And once things had calmed down, and he was riding home with his family, he kept wondering why he wasn't very happy.

When he got home, he went upstairs to his room. He sat on the floor and leaned against his bed. His back was still hurting some, but he didn't think about that.

He ran the game back through his mind. He pictured his big run. And he thought about the power move he had made to get to the goal line on the two-point play.

But he also remembered the confusion and the panic he had felt. He knew he had been very lucky to escape the rush on his touchdown run.

He was thinking about all the mistakes he had made when his dad came to the door.

"Sterling, you look like you *lost* the game," he said. "What's bothering you?"

Dad wouldn't want to hear it, but Sterling told

the truth. "I still feel like I'd rather not be the quarterback."

Mr. Malone walked over to Sterling's desk. He turned the chair around and sat down. Then he leaned over and took a hard look at Sterling. "Why?" he asked.

"I made some good runs. But my passes were lousy. I can throw the ball all right in practice. But I panic when I get out there on the field."

"Well, sure. Kenny is having the same problem. You both need more experience, that's all."

"It's not just that."

"What else?"

"What if I had gotten sacked instead of breaking loose on that run? What if we had lost? Everyone would be blaming me right now instead of calling me the hero."

"That's right. The quarterback takes a lot of credit—more than he deserves—when a team wins. And he takes a lot of criticism when the team loses. That's just the way it is."

"I don't like it, Dad. I feel good when I'm carrying the ball. I just react and don't have to think. But at quarterback, I have a million things to worry about."

Mr. Malone looked down at the floor. He

shook his head. "A black kid in this country should never, *ever* think that way," he said.

"Come on, Dad. Don't start all that. This isn't about being black. I just want to play the position I'm best at."

"No, son. That's where you're wrong."

Sterling knew it was coming now. One of Dad's speeches.

"Sterling, my great-great-grandfather was a slave."

This was the speech, all right.

"When one man *owns* another man, how do you think he lives with himself? How does he justify it in his own mind?"

But this was something new. Sterling had never really thought much about it. "I don't know," he said.

"Well, the owner has to tell himself that the man he owns is not a *real* human being. He's *stupid.* He's like the mule that the man also owns. Do you understand what I'm saying?"

"Yeah."

"Well, okay. Those people didn't stop thinking that way overnight. A lot of people *still* think that way. To them, the African American can be a good running back. That takes speed and strength. But he can't play quarterback. That takes *brains.*"

"Not many people think that any more, Dad."

"I hope you're right. But there's still too many who do. And that's why we have to keep fighting for our rightful place."

Sterling let out his breath. "Why can't people just be people? Why do we always have to prove something?"

"I can't change what is, son. And that's how things are."

"Kenny's Hispanic. He needs to fight for his people too." Sterling smiled. "Can't I let him have *his* chance?"

"I have no problem with that, son. If the boy is better than you, that's fine. I just don't want you hanging your head and saying you can't take the heat."

Sterling thought it all over.

"Okay," he said, finally. "I'll keep trying. But I just don't think anyone cares whether some kid in Angel Park plays quarterback or not. It's not as big a deal as you're making it."

"Sterling, we win one little battle at a time. Your teammates—from all races—will remember the black kid who was not just a good player but a team leader. A thinker."

"Reggie plays quarterback. It's not like the world changed any because of that."

"It changed a little, Sterling. Ever so little. But

it changed. I really believe that."

Sterling wondered.

"Son, when I was in high school, I *wanted* to try out for quarterback. The coach told me I'd make a better running back. And I knew exactly what he was thinking. Now you have your shot. It's important you don't back away from it."

About then Reggie stepped to door.

"Are you getting the 'black guys gotta try harder' speech?" he asked.

Sterling looked up.

Reggie was smiling.

"Yeah," Sterling said. "It turns out, if I get to be quarterback, the world will be a better place."

He glanced over at his dad. "You got that right," Dad said. And then he smiled too.

"And you won't get any pity from me," Reggie said. "Because I believe he's right."

Sterling suddenly felt proud of his dad and brother.

"Well, I'll do my best," he said.

"And you know what?" Reggie said. "I've got a feeling your best might be better than mine. You've got the ability, Sterling. You can be *great*."

"I can run okay. But I can't pass," Sterling said.

"You can pass. You just have to relax. Once you do, you're going to be *something*."

Sterling had always believed he was second-rate compared to his big brother—who was a great athlete at every sport he played. All this was a surprise to him.

"Thanks, Reggie," he said.

He told himself that he was going to quit complaining about playing quarterback.

He was going to give it his best shot.

★8★

The Ball Is Yours

At the next practice Coach Mahana called Kenny and Sterling aside. He was holding a football under his arm.

"I gotta tell you the truth," he said. "Neither one of you played very well against Blue Springs. We were lucky to win."

Both boys nodded.

"You both seemed scared to take control and lead the team. Malone, you didn't throw a decent pass in the whole game. You lost your cool every time you got chased a little."

"I know."

"But I guess you're going to be the quarter-back. I'm going to start you in the next game."

After what the coach had just said, Sterling was shocked.

"At least in this last game, Malone played a little better than you did, Sandoval."

"Do you still want me to be the backup quarterback?" Kenny asked. Sterling didn't really hear any disappointment in his voice.

"Well, yeah. But you're too good an athlete to be standing on the sidelines. So I want you to trade off with Peter and Cosel at wide receiver. And then, if Sterling can't get the job done at quarterback, I'll go back to you."

"Okay."

"So, Sterling, you get the ball." The coach held it out. "Do something with it."

"Okay."

"Hey, I know you can run. But you gotta be the leader out there. You have to make believers out of your team. You've got a good head on your shoulders, but you've got to use it."

"I know."

"All right. Let's go play some football."

And that's what the coach told the players again on Thursday when they got ready to go out on the field. This was the last practice game.

"I still haven't seen you guys play *football*," he said. "You won a game and, I'll admit, you played some good defense. But I want to see you put a complete game together."

It was another one of those speeches.

But Sterling was feeling a little different about that stuff today. He had made up his mind that he was going to lead the way.

"I'll tell you something else," the coach was saying. "These kids from Cactus Hills are always tough. They're well coached, and they *hit*. If you think you can win today without going all out, you're kidding yourselves."

The Cactus Hills team was called the Bull-dozers.

And the name fit.

They rarely threw the ball. They lined up and pounded the ball on the ground. And the only way to stop them was to meet their power with power.

The quarterback was a pretty good athlete—a guy named Higdon. But the real star was a big fullback named Manny Tovar.

Sterling had watched the Bulldozers play the week before. Tovar had carried the ball about three-fourths of the time.

And the kid had never stopped driving ahead.

He had some good moves, but he was mainly a powerhouse. It always took two or three guys to get him down.

Sterling knew what that meant. Once someone had slowed Tovar down, the backs would have to come up and pound him.

And yet the defensive backs couldn't get caught out of position. Once in a while the Bulldozers would pass, just to keep the defenders honest.

The Bulldozers won the toss and chose to receive.

Their first play from scrimmage was a slam-bam run into the line.

The linemen hit like trucks, and Tovar sliced for five. Then he dragged two guys for another four.

Second and 1.

The next play was a smash-it-in-your-face run up the middle.

Tovar got the first down and kept struggling for three more.

Coach Mahana was sputtering and shouting. "Are you guys going to play football, or are you going to stand around and *watch*?"

Sterling told himself he had to close sooner. "Come on, you guys," he shouted. "Let's fire out this time."

And they did.

But Tovar still got five.

"Come on, let's stop 'em right there. Get that guy!" Brett shouted.

Sterling told himself to be careful. "Don't forget about the receivers," he yelled.

But when Higdon faked to Tovar, the linebackers all pulled in for the run up the middle.

Higdon turned and pitched out to the running back, who went wide.

Sterling had stayed home.

He broke toward the running back, but he was all alone out there. He had to stay under control and not get juked.

He made the sure tackle—and saved a big gainer. But the running back had picked up six and made the first down.

And now the defense had to think about more than just Tovar. Sterling knew they were in for a tough game.

The Bulldozers kept moving the same way. A couple of times the Sidewinders held their own up front, and they stopped Tovar for no gain—or a short one.

But the Bulldozers never panicked. They knew what they could do. They just bashed ahead all the harder the next time.

The march never stopped. Cactus Hills didn't pass once, and they only ran outside a couple of times.

They simply played smash-face football, and they drove all the way to the end zone. The place kicker hit the extra point, and the Bulldozers were ahead 7 to 0.

Sterling was nervous during the kickoff that followed. He knew he had to answer.

The Sidewinder offense had to show the Bulldozers that another team was out there.

Sterling was glad when the coach called a pass on the first play of the series. This was a tough team, but not a fast one. Maybe the Bulldozers would have trouble with a passing attack.

Cosel ran a nice route. He faked his defender and angled over the middle.

Sterling stood his ground and fired.

He hit Cosel right in the hands.

Fifteen yards!

Suddenly Sterling felt good. He felt himself relax.

He looked his players in the eyes. "All right. We can move the ball on these guys. Block hard. Split right. Eighty-three pass. On two. *Yo!*"

Cosel took his man deep this time, and Sterling hit Peter on the underneath pattern. Peter had some room, and he ran for another first down.

Sterling heard the Bulldozer defensive backs

yelling back and forth. He heard the worry in their voices. Now the shoe was on the other foot.

Sterling felt his confidence. He knew the team could feel it too.

The coach sent in a running play—a smash of their own.

But it was strength against strength, and the Cactus Hills line didn't budge. They slammed the door on Derek at the line of scrimmage.

Sterling ran a roll-out, looping to the right side. Then he passed for seven yards. But now the Sidewinders were looking at third and 3.

The coach called for the eighty pass—the curl pattern. The receivers would run downfield, stop suddenly, and turn back toward Sterling for the pass.

Sterling dropped back and saw the rush coming. But he didn't panic. He stayed still as Derek blocked a crashing linebacker.

Peter was open on the left side. Wide open. Sterling tossed a perfect pass, right at his chest.

But Peter started to turn before he made the catch. He took his eye off the ball. It hit him in the chest and bounced away.

The drive was over, just when Sterling had thought everything was going so well.

But the offensive players knew they could

move the ball. Now they just had to stop the Bulldozers.

But it didn't happen.

Cactus Hills started on its own 25-yard line.
And once again they smashed and banged their
way up the field.

Sterling came up once to stop a sweep, with
Tovar leading the blocking. The guy lowered a
shoulder and knocked Sterling right on his rear
end.

Sterling got up with his head feeling fuzzy. His
hand was hurting where it had gotten smashed
between his body and Tovar's shoulder pads.

But mostly his pride was hurting.

These guys were showing the Sidewinders how
to play.

And the drive kept going.

Finally Tovar pounded through the line and
flattened Matthew Kincade.

Sterling charged in to help, but Tovar gave
him a fake, and made a great cut.

Sterling tackled nothing but air.

When he jumped up, he could see that Tovar
had done the same thing to Tucker.

And that was it.

Tovar high-stepped his way into the end zone,
then turned around and did a little dance.

Sterling wanted to go dance on his chest for a while.

But he knew the truth.

The guy was good. And his own team had to start hitting or it was going to be too late.

The place kicker hit the ball through the uprights again, and the Bulldozers were ahead, 14 to 0.

★9★

Think!

Tucker made a good return on the kickoff—back almost to the 40-yard line.

The offense took over.

Before the first play from scrimmage, Sterling looked at his teammates. "Hey, you guys, they're not bigger than we are. They're just hitting harder. We've got to turn *that* around."

It sounded like one of those things his dad would say.

Or the coach.

But Sterling believed it.

"Split right. Dive right. On set. Now let's *hit them!*"

The Sidewinders hurried up to the line. Maybe the defense was playing a little loose, thinking pass.

But Tucker hit the line and popped through. He picked up 16 yards before the defensive backs could run him down.

Then Derek hit up the middle. And he picked up seven.

The line was *blocking*.

Then the coach called a play-action pass.

Perfect!

Sterling faked to Derek and put the ball on his hip as he dropped back. Derek carried out the fake, and the defense bought the run.

Cosel streaked past the cornerback and was open, long.

Sterling set his feet and let the ball fly. And the pass was on the money.

But *just* a little long!

Even with all his speed, Cosel couldn't quite run under it. Six points had been waiting, and Sterling had missed again.

But he told the players, "Don't worry. We've got 'em guessing now. Next time we get a guy open, I won't miss him."

But as it turned out, it was the option play that broke big. It was the first play of the second quarter.

Sterling ran left and faked a cut upfield. He drew in the defense and then hit Tucker with the pitch.

Tucker raced past the two defenders who hit Sterling, and then he cut back against the pursuit.

He put a fake on the safety and was off to the races.

No one touched him all the way to the end zone.

The Sidewinders were happy to get the score. But there was a lot of work left to do. Everyone looked determined.

Harlan had been working hard on his place-kicking all week. The coach decided to kick for one point.

And Harlan booted it through.

The score was 14 to 7. The Sidewinders were starting to believe.

But more than anything, the defense had to stop Cactus Hills this time.

Sterling shouted to his fellow defenders, "Let's meet 'em head-on. Let's see who the power team is."

But on the very first play, Tovar hammered through the line and picked up eight yards.

And on the next play he drove straight ahead again.

No...

It was a fake.

The quarterback had kept the ball. Now he

was looping a pass to the wide receiver on Sterling's side of the field.

But Sterling had expected something like that. He had even seen something in the receiver's eyes.

He charged the receiver. Just as the ball hit the guy's hands, Sterling's shoulder smacked into his gut.

He *slammed* the receiver, and the ball slipped away.

Sterling heard the receiver suck air, and he heard the players on the Bulldozer sideline let out a moan.

The receiver got up in a few seconds—but he wouldn't forget Sterling.

The defense all charged over and slapped Sterling on the helmet. Now they were *on fire.* "What a hit!" Sterling heard his teammates shouting. "Let's shut 'em down right here."

It was third and 2, not much for Tovar to pick up.

But the defensive line drove forward like a row of tanks. Tovar hit the line and bounced back.

He tried to spin and take the play wide, but Kenny came up fast. He *bashed* Tovar in the chest and drove him back.

Sterling heard the pop of Kenny's shoulder pads all the way across the field.

Tovar got up slowly, and then he walked off the field.

He wasn't dancing now.

For the first time the Bulldozers had to punt.

But they didn't back away from the fight.

In fact, the rest of the half was a battle of hard-smashing defenses. And the third quarter went the same way.

Toward the end of the quarter, Sterling led the team on a good drive. He hit some short passes, and the option worked.

But the drive bogged down when the Bulldozer defense broke through and sacked him on a third and 6.

Early in the fourth quarter, the Bulldozers started opening up a little more. They threw a couple of passes that worked.

And then the quarterback threw to a wide receiver behind the line of scrimmage.

But the ball hit the ground. The receiver caught it on one bounce. Then he shook his head and looked disgusted.

At the same moment Coach Mahana screamed, "The ball's alive! Don't stop."

Sterling suddenly realized what the coach

meant. The "pass" had been backwards—a lateral. It could be picked up. The play wasn't over.

About that time the wide receiver cocked his arm to throw.

The play was a trick.

Sterling spun and raced down the field. The tight end had slipped away from his defender and was wide open.

The pass was not great—a lob. And the tight end had to wait for it. Otherwise, it would have gone for a touchdown.

Sterling's speed took him over the ground quickly. He caught the tight end just inside the 20.

The defense really had to rise up and do something now or the Bulldozers would put the game away.

The Bulldozers went back to their power on the first play. But the Sidewinders *stuffed* Tovar for a short loss.

Then Cactus Hills tried to go wide, but Lee Makosh broke through the line and threw the running back for another loss.

On third down, Higdon went back to pass. Just as he tried to set himself, Billy blasted him.

And put him on his back!

Billy jumped up and did an awkward little

dance—his copy of the one Tovar had done in the end zone.

And now it was fourth down.

The Bulldozers tried another trick—a running-back pass. But the Sidewinders didn't fall for the fake run.

The back had to eat the ball and take another loss.

So the Sidewinders took over on downs. Now it was time to make the offense work again.

Sterling told the players, "Okay, we're going all the way this time. This might be our last chance."

Sterling kept the ball on an option and got four yards.

Then he dumped a pass over the middle to Josh for seven.

First down.

The line fired out and gave Derek a big hole. He picked up five yards.

And then Kenny came into the game for Peter at wide receiver. Sterling hit him on a sideline pass for seven yards.

First down.

The Sidewinders were into Bulldozer territory—on the 43-yard line.

The play came in. Another give to Derek. The

coach was mixing up the plays well. And the line was driving hard.

But this time the defense was ready. Derek got only a yard.

So Angel Park went back to the sideline pass, this time to the right side.

The pass was on target, and Cosel made the catch. But the cornerback made a great tackle and kept Cosel two yards short of the first down.

Crunch time. Third and 2.

"Option right" was the call again.

But Sterling saw the defense loading up for the play. They were looking for it.

He called time out and ran to the sideline.

"Coach, they're expecting the option," he said.

"Okay. Good. I'm glad you saw it. Maybe we should go with play action and hit Josh."

"We did that earlier. They'll be watching Josh."

"So what do you think we ought to do?"

"We've been hitting that sideline pass. If I pump fake, and the receiver breaks long, I think we can beat the cornerback."

"Maybe we better get the first down and then try that."

"Yeah. But that's what they're thinking too. They don't expect us to go long."

"Okay. But the pass has to be there."

"It'll be there."

"Do you want to go left or right?"

"Left. The guy on the right is playing Cosel a little loose. But the guy on Kenny is coming up tight. And Kenny's faster than Peter. He'll surprise his defender."

"Okay. Sterling, that's the kind of stuff you have to notice. Now you're being the leader."

Sterling nodded and turned to go.

But the coach grabbed him by the arm. "Just hit the pass."

Sterling didn't worry about it. He was too psyched right now to think of making a mistake. And he was having fun.

In the huddle he told Kenny to make a good fake, and wait for the pump fake before he broke.

And that's just what Kenny did.

He drew in the cornerback, then broke past him. And he darted down the sideline.

Everything had worked—except that a lineman slipped off a block and broke through. He was falling, but he grabbed Sterling by the leg.

Sterling pulled loose and bounced to the left.

A linebacker was twisting off a block and trying to get to him.

Kenny had seen that Sterling was in trouble and had broken toward the middle of the field.

He was all alone.

Sterling brought back his arm and fired.

But he took a big hit as he released the ball. He was on his back when he heard his teammates cheer. He jumped up just in time to see Kenny race across the goal line.

Sterling ran all the way to the end zone to slap hands with Kenny.

But there was still work to do. Sterling knew the coach would never settle for a tie. The Sidewinders needed to prove to themselves that they could smash heads with a tough team—and come out on top.

The coach called for a roll-out pass. The receivers would all get to the end zone and break right. Sterling would run to the right and look for the open guy.

As Sterling called the play, he could feel his voice shake a little. He was nervous, but he wasn't scared. Somehow, he would get this done.

He took the snap and rolled to the right. Josh slipped into the open in the end zone.

But just as Sterling was about to let the ball fly, the strong safety came up hard on Josh. Sterling waited.

He waved the ball in the air to show the defense he intended to pass, and then he saw his chance. He pulled the ball down and bulled toward the end zone.

But a linebacker smashed into him at the 1-yard line. Sterling lowered his shoulder and took the blow. Then he spun hard—and dove for the white line.

He reached with the ball as he went down—his arms stretched all the way out.

As he slammed onto his chest, he felt the wind go out of him. He wasn't sure if he had made it.

But he rolled over quickly and saw a referee with both arms in the air.

Two points!

The Sidewinders had the lead, 15 to 14.

And there was no messing with them after that. They played defense like wild men. And the offense pushed ahead for enough first downs to eat up the clock.

When it was all over, Sterling felt as though he were one big bruise. And his knees didn't want to hold him up. When his teammates mobbed him, he got knocked right off his feet.

Kenny finally pulled him up. "Hey, I like it like this. I like *catching* the passes and *scoring* the touchdowns."

The coach grabbed them both around the shoulders. His huge arms pulled them in against his sides. "Hey, I found a quarterback today," he said. "*And* a great pass combination. You two showed me some leadership—on offense *and* defense."

Sterling was laughing, but he said, "I think maybe I changed the world a little. That's what I think."

Coach Mahana looked a little confused. But Sterling was looking past him at his dad, who was running forward to grab him. "You got that right," his father said.

And Reggie was right behind his dad. "Hey, the world's a whole new place, if you ask me," he said, laughing.

Sterling smiled at his dad and brother. "Well, let's say, a *slightly* different place," he said. He believed it too.

And he was suddenly very happy to be the quarterback.

Glossary

blitz   A play in which one or more defensive players charge ahead just as the ball is hiked in an attempt to make an early tackle. This is often done when the defense suspects that the offensive team will pass the ball.

block   An attempt by an offensive player to keep a defender from getting past him to make a tackle. The offensive player may use his shoulders or body, but he may not grab the defender or hold him with his arms.

center   The player in the center of the offensive line. He hikes the ball to the quarterback.

PAT   "Point after touchdown," also called the "extra point," or a "conversion." One point may be scored by place-kicking the ball through the goal posts. Two points may be scored by running or passing the ball into the end zone.

cornerbacks   Defensive backfield players who are assigned to cover wide receivers on passing plays.

counter play   A running play in which the quarterback fakes a handoff to one back and then hands off to another, who angles to the opposite side of the line from the first back.

curl pattern   A route run by a receiver. He begins to run hard, as though he will continue straight down the field, but then he stops and turns back toward the quarterback to receive a pass.

defensive ends Defensive linemen who are positioned at the ends of the line.

dive play A running play in which an offensive backfield player takes a handoff from the quarterback and quickly plunges through a hole in the line.

down Each offensive play is called a "down." The offensive team must gain ten yards in four plays—downs—or give up the ball to the defense.

end zone A rectangular area at each end of the field. A touchdown is scored when a player with the ball runs into the end zone or catches a pass inside it.

field goal A scoring kick. The ball must be kicked from the ground, and it must pass over the cross bar on the goal post, and between the two uprights. A field goal counts for three points.

formation The positioning of offensive players. Each team uses various formations in an attempt to confuse the defense.

forward pass Usually called simply a "pass," this is any throw from one player to another that travels ahead of the player who makes the throw. Such a throw is only legal behind the line of scrimmage.

fly pattern A hard straight run down the field made by a receiver, who hopes to run past all defenders and catch a long pass.

fullback An offensive backfield player. He is usually a powerful runner who can make yardage running through the line.

guards Offensive players who line up left and right of the center. Their primary job is to block for the backs. Also, defensive players who line up across from offensive guards.

hole Space created by offensive blockers so that an offensive back can get through the line on a running play.

huddle The grouping of players just before a play. The quarterback or defensive captain calls the offensive play or defensive formation.

kickoff The play that begins a football game. A player kicks the ball while it is on a kicking tee, on the ground. The player who receives the ball may run back with it until he is tackled. If the ball reaches the end zone, the receiver may choose not to run with the ball and then the offensive team starts its first play from its own 20-yard line. After each score in a football game, the scoring team kicks off to start play again.

lead blocker An offensive player who runs ahead of a ball carrier and attempts to block defenders.

linebackers Defensive players who position themselves just behind the defensive linemen. They must be able to cover both running plays and passes.

linemen   Players on offense and defense who line up at the line of scrimmage at the start of a play. These include the offensive center and the offensive and defensive guards, tackles, and ends.

line of scrimmage   The imaginary line straight across from the ball. The offense and defense must line up on opposite sides of this line before each play begins.

motion penalty   A loss of yardage for an offensive team for moving before the ball is hiked. One player may "go in motion" before the ball is hiked, but only if he is moving across the field and not toward the line of scrimmage.

off-tackle run   An offensive play in which the offensive line tries to open a hole just outside one of the tackles, so that an offensive back can carry the ball through.

option play   Any play in which offensive players have the choice to take different actions. The most common option play goes to the quarterback, who first has the option to hand off to the fullback or keep the ball, and then has the option to lateral to a trailing back or again keep the ball.

pitch   Also called a "pitch out" or a "lateral," this is a throw in which the quarterback or other player tosses the ball to a player who is even with or behind him.

place-kick   A field goal or PAT (extra point) kick. The ball must be kicked from the ground and is held in place by another player.

punt A kick in which the punter drops the ball and then kicks it before it touches the ground. This is usually done on fourth down when the offensive team has little chance of gaining a first down. It is a way of giving up the ball to the defense as far down the field as possible.

quarterback The offensive backfield player who calls the plays and receives the ball first from the center. The quarterback may hand the ball off, pass it, or run with it himself.

reverse play A running play in which an offensive back begins to run around one end of the line, only to hand off to a player who reverses the field and runs around the opposite end.

roll-out An offensive play in which the quarterback loops wide to pass rather than staying behind the line. The play also opens up the option to run if defensive players stay back to cover the pass.

running back An offensive backfield player who often carries the ball on running plays. Running backs may also receive passes.

rush The attempt of defensive players to break through blocks and tackle the quarterback before he can pass the ball.

sack A tackle of a quarterback behind the line of scrimmage before he is able to throw a pass, causing the offensive team a loss of yardage.

safety   The defensive backfield player who covers long passes.

sideline pass   A pass thrown to a receiver who darts straight ahead and then cuts to the sideline. The quarterback attempts to throw the ball just as the player cuts and just before he goes out of bounds.

strong safety   A defensive backfield player who is normally assigned to cover the tight end on pass plays.

sweep   A running play in which an offensive backfield player, led by blockers, attempts to run around the end of the line.

tackle   Offensive players who line up outside the guards. Their primary job is to block for the backs. Also, defensive players who line up across from offensive tackles. "Tackle" is also the term used for knocking an offensive player off his feet.

tight ends   Offensive players who line up outside the tackles. Often, only one tight end plays at a time, and lines up either at the right or left end of the line. Tight ends are blockers, but they also receive passes.

touchdown   A six-point score received when an offensive player crosses into the end zone with the ball or catches a pass in the end zone.

wide receivers   Offensive backfield players who usually line up wide to the left or right of the line and one yard back from the line of scrimmage. Their primary job is to receive passes.

DEAN HUGHES has written many books for children, including the popular *Nutty* stories and *Jelly's Circus*. He has also published such works of literary fiction for young adults as the highly acclaimed *Family Pose*. Writing keeps Mr. Hughes very busy, but he does find time to run and play golf—and he loves to watch almost all sports. His home is in Utah. He and his wife have three children.

Play ball with the kids from Angel Park!

ANGEL PARK ALL-STARS™

by Dean Hughes

Meet Kenny, Harlan, and Jacob—three talented young rookies on Angel Park's Little League team. They're in for plenty of hard-hitting fastball action...as well as fun and friendship. You'll want to read them all!

BULLSEYE BOOKS PUBLISHED BY RANDOM HOUSE, INC.

The all-star soccer action starts here!

Angel Park
SOCCER STARS™

by Dean Hughes

Jacob Scott is back with some new friends and a whole new sport—soccer. Join the Angel Park Pride as they pass, shoot, and score their way toward the league championship in an exciting series filled with the same nonstop action as the Angel Park All-Stars. You'll want them all for your collection!

BULLSEYE BOOKS PUBLISHED BY RANDOM HOUSE, INC.

Plenty of slam-dunk action!

ANGEL PARK HOOP STARS™

by Dean Hughes

The all-star athletes from Angel Park are back—and they're scoring big points on the basketball court. Join Miles, Harlan, and the rest of the Hoop Stars as they face the opposition head-on and work their way toward victory. Filled with lots of fast-paced basketball excitement and high-scoring fun!

BULLSEYE BOOKS PUBLISHED BY RANDOM HOUSE, INC.